Praise for *The Ghost of Iris Carver*

If there were ever any doubts in my mind about Alanna Rusnak's extraordinary talent, she has fully eradicated any uncertainty with her latest novella, *The Ghost of Iris Carver*. Not only was she able to create deeply engaging characters and bring them fully to life on the page, but she was equally capable of expertly placing them into a conceptual labyrinth and concealing them just behind the venerable, sacred, fourth wall.

> —Geraldine Mac Donald, medical translator,
> writer, published author

A beautiful reminder of why I love (Alanna's) writing.

> —William F. Aicher, author of *The Unfortunate Expiration of
> David S. Sparks* and *A Confession*

The Ghost of Iris Carver is a beautifully woven farewell love letter to the quirky Iris I fell in love with in *The Church in the Wildwood*.

> —Heidi Eastman, early reader

The emotions of the characters are tangible... there is an understanding of not only how the character feels, but why... The author is successful in making sure the reader isn't just a witness to the events unfolding before them. They are instead drawn into the emotion to feel... as the character feels. This gives the characters a dimensionality that makes them come alive to the reader.

> —Michelle McLaughlin, assistant editor, *Blank Spaces* Magazine

Alanna paints with words. I feel like her characters are my family.

> —Patricia Manale, early reader

Praise for *The Church in the Wildwood*

This novel is hauntingly imagined and gorgeously told. It immediately surrounded me with a mood that lingered almost heavily, while the intriguing and layered plot made it an absolute page-turner! *The Church in the Wildwood* is expertly and thoughtfully crafted, an impressive recipe of poetry and plot - it captivated me with beautiful phrasing that begged attention while twists, turns, and soul-searching characters compelled me to quickly read on. The author offers a heart-wrenching and dangerous story - child abuse and unfathomable family secrets appear throughout - yet she weaves it all together with thoughtful insights that keep the reader hopeful. I found it easy to understand and care for the vast array of entangled characters who are offered their own space to falter, fail, and try again. This is a fantastic and emotional read!

—Tsara Shelton, *author of Spinning in Circles and Learning From Myself*

Gorgeous and meaningful story! A wonderful plot that takes the reader on a deep journey with real-life struggles and an inspiring, realistic portrayal of abuse and relationships. *The Church in the Wildwood* is not in-your-face religious or preachy: I'm an atheist and was totally engaged and enjoyed the book! The story leaves you feeling touched and inspired. Highly recommend!

—Pamela Hopwood, freelance writer, assistant editor, *Blank Spaces* Magazine

Alanna is such a lovely writer, her words are poetic and tragic but filled with hope. She deals with real darkness in *The Church in the Wildwood* but does so in such a beautiful way.

—Kristina Dyck, blogger

Following a tragic accident, the tortured past of Joseph's mother is brought to light. How much of Joseph's history has been distorted through her deception? Does her past as an abused, child-bride in a polygamist cult excuse her sins? Does the camp fire story about his father's suicide hold any truth? What really happened the day he was born? A deeply evocative story, *The Church in the Wildwood* presents humanity at both its best and worst. The depth and authenticity of each character is a triumph to say the least. It takes great skill to create characters so flawed, yet relatable. Although the story moves slowly at first, the ever increasing plot tension draws the reader in, refusing release until the very last page. A poignant beauty, that can exist in the ugliest corners of the world, is presented artfully by the author. This could have been a very heavy coming of age story, as it touches on abuse and death. Rather than creating another version of the tired "poor, little orphan" plot line, the imagery and unique perspective has created a story of love, forgiveness and spirituality in a fallen world. Although harsh, the story is depicted through a fresh lens of redemption and hope, reminiscent of the innocence conveyed in the book *Room* by Emma Donoghue. While the plot line is engaging, the skillfully woven internal conflict and personal growth of each character is the true focal point of the book. The reader is taken on a journey from a place of judgement to compassion as the story unfolds, reminding us that everyone has a backstory and it is wrong to condemn someone without walking a mile in their shoes. We each need a church in the wildwood, where we can forgive the past and say goodbye to the memories and relics that haunt us.

—Dawn Edgcumbe, Amazon reviewer

Such a gifted writer. (*The Church in the Wildwood*) is like a gift I'm slowly unwrapping.

—Diane Samson, writer

the ghost of iris carver

Alanna Rusnak

Other titles in The Fallmoore Chronicles

The Church in the Wildwood
The Ghost of Iris Carver
Black Bird (coming soon)

Cover design by Alanna Rusnak
Photography courtesy of pixabay.com

THE GHOST OF IRIS CARVER

A Fallmoore Chronicles Novella

Alanna Rusnak

2018

 First Printing: 2018
ALANNA RUSNAK PUBLISHING

Blake, Oscar. *Vacant Space*. Used with permission from the author.

Hemingway, Ernest. *For Whom the Bell Tolls*. New York: Charles Scribner's Sons, 1940. Print, public domain.

Rusnak, Alanna. *The Church in the Wildwood*. Alanna Rusnak Publishing, 2017. Print.

Tennyson, Alfred Tennyson, Baron. "*Ring Out, Wild Bells*" Boston: Lee and Shepard, 1883. Print, public domain.

ISBN 13: 978-0-9959907-4-6
ISBN 10: 0995990743

Alanna Rusnak Publishing
282906 Normanby/Bentinck Townline
Durham, Ontario, Canada, N0G 1R0
www.publishing.alannarusnak.com

Contact publisher for Library and Archives Catalogue information

for Iris

everything is real

I drew your shape in the snow
And laid down beside it.
Looking up past the stars
at the surrounding universe
I realized that I felt there
still was a whole lot of you
in a whole lot of nothing.

Oscar Blake
Vacant Space

"There she was in the Queen Anne's Lace and the puddle that showed the reflection of the sun; in the grass that fought its way through the gravel shoulder; in the birds that flew overhead, their songs an anthem to a life without worry. Her fingers slid through his hair as the wind whipped his weary body and he heard her voice, forever and always, whispering the Psalms as the road passed beneath him."

—The Church in the Wildwood, page 112

"She wished to move with the grace of a ghost— all whispers and secrets and sighs."

—The Church in the Wildwood, page 69

IRIS (nee Callum) CARVER, age 33 of Fallmoore, Ontario passed away quietly at the Fallmoore General Hospital on July 9, 1977. Born to MARGARET (Lyndsay) and BRUCE CALLUM of Harridan Point on August 17, 1944, Iris was baptized into the Harridan Church of the Nazarene when she was six months old.

Iris is predeceased by her husband, Paisley Carver of Carver Alfalfa, and survived by her only child, Joseph — sole heir to Mr. Carver's land and business.

No service was held on request of the family. Gestures of condolence may be forwarded as donations in Iris' name to the Fallmoore Library.

chapter one
room key

April 2018

THE FALLMOORE MOTEL STOOD AT THE top of the hill, its shabby exterior further darkened by the shadow of the First Presbyterian Church as the sun crept below the western horizon each evening.

The dusty grey building was the only option for overnight guests in the small town, offering a long stretch of teal doors, brass numbers, and fifty-five dollar rooms that still used actual keys. The shag carpet and polyester drapes added a tired charm, but the mattress seemed new, and the linens were deliciously fresh.

I sat against a pile of pillows, coffee from the in-room single-cup machine sitting under the lamp on the little table beside me, steaming weakly against the yellow halo created by the incandescent bulb. The red glow of the alarm clock told me it was nearly six o'clock in the morning.

Though exhausted, my night had been restless, the bed now strewn with the evidence of my vocation: laptop, notebooks, random scribbles on motel stationary.

I had dreamed of being a writer since my father brought home a black Olympian typewriter in 1989 and taught me the proper placement for my fingers. I held tight to the knowledge of my realized dream, and I revelled in the shelves of my own name, touching my titles with the same awe as when I placed my hands on those heavy black keys as a nine year old girl.

Anxiety plagued me. Creating a world and visiting it were two very different things. I didn't know if I was ready to learn what I'd come to discover.

I didn't know if I was ready to let go.

THE CHURCH BELL RANG JUST AS THE SUN began to leak through a small break in the curtains. It caused a catch in my throat as I felt it in my bones, my body absorbing those storied notes, my eyes burning at the memory of all who'd heard them before me. I rubbed my temples with a finger and thumb and I leaned back against the headboard, sighing.

"You been here before?" the elderly woman at the counter had asked me the night before when I checked in.

"No," I'd said. "Not really." And I hadn't been. Not *really*. Not physically, though my heart had been there a thousand times since I wrote the first story of this town.

"What brings you here then?" she asked.

"I'm meeting a friend," I told her, and she'd nodded with a raised eyebrow like it was some sort of scandal.

I nursed my coffee as the final notes of the bell faded into the morning air, making the drink last until the sun had fully risen and I was completely awake.

I felt the tug of the phone book and I chewed my lip as I tried to fight it, knowing I'd give in because I knew myself too well. I set my mug back on the nightstand, coffee nothing but a memory staining the bottom. I pulled the drawer open, seeing the Eastern Bodensee White Pages sitting pristine and stoic beside the Gideon Bible.

I could have used my smartphone to find what I was looking for but that seemed wrong, given the history I held with this place. I'd left it in my purse, ringer off, tossed on the threadbare occasional chair so as not to mar the memory of the simpler times this room had known.

I saw myself reflected in the rounded glass of the old television set sitting on the dresser against the far wall. I squinted my eyes, allowing my image to melt into the 1970s technology. I'd always thought I was born in the wrong decade. Wood decals and orange accents felt like home to me.

I pulled the 2011 phone book onto my lap and flipped it open to the C's. It was seven years old; but, like everything else in this tired town, I was sure little had changed within. It lay across my thighs like a paper tidal wave and I almost felt the movement of an ocean as I ran my finger down the column, landing beside his name.

Carver, J.

My body froze and I sucked in my breath, terrified and exhilarated in the same moment, picking up the phone before I had time to recognize what I was doing.

"No," I chastised myself. "No. Not yet." I settled the receiver back into its cradle.

I left the phone book on the side table with my empty mug and stepped into the shower.

SOMEONE WAS KNOCKING ON MY DOOR WHEN I turned off the water. I wrapped a towel around my dripping body and cracked the door open. The woman from the check-in counter stood there.

"Yes?"

"Morning," she said. "There's breakfast for you if you like. In the room beside the office. You and your friend are welcome to it."

I let the door open a little wider to show the empty room. "It's just me," I told her.

She nodded and looked past me to the bed and its disarray of sheets. "Yeah?" she said.

"Just me," I said again. "Thanks."

Small towns. They're the same everywhere.

WITH MY HAIR STILL WET, I PUSHED OPEN THE door to room number one. Its layout was exactly like my own but it had no bed. Instead, one long folding table held the breakfast spoils. There were no other tables or chairs.

I eyed the options, disturbed by the cereal bowl full of hardboiled eggs. I pushed a piece of bread into the toaster and shoved two jam packets into my pocket before I helped myself to another cup of coffee from the machine beside the toaster.

Back in my room, I smeared jam across the multigrain bread and took a bite as I lingered over the phone book again. *What would he say if he knew I was here?*

This was Joseph Carver's town. It had been since his mother left it to him.

Of course, it wasn't *his*. Not in the way a person has a thing. But it was his in the way a place forever belongs to the person who made it matter to you. Because it had been *hers*. And she was the reason for everything, wasn't she? And he was what she left behind. Her shadow. Her legacy. Her lingering breath, fogging over the glass of this place so that you must rub through her to see anything beyond. I wondered if I would leave that kind of residue in my wake. It's what we all want in some form or another. Though I don't know that I'd choose fog. I'd rather glimmer from a stream, or bow with the wheat, golden beneath a summer sun.

She wanted to be remembered in sunlight. I wished for the same.

There was no Fallmoore without Joseph. No town without the tragic history of his little family; as if it existed for the sole purpose of containing his narrative. And, in a way, I suppose that's the truth of it. His fate is stamped on me like a second skin, tattooed upon my guilty palette.

He'd be 55 or 56 now, having seen forty years since his story touched mine. I wondered if he still felt the loss of his family with the same potency as in those first days. Grief has a way of loosening its hold without ever really letting go. And time travel has no power over the grip of loss.

I hoped for his happiness, and thought, surely, my own depended on it.

I STEPPED OUT ON THE CRACKED SIDEWALK that would lead me to our meeting place. The cool air fired a shiver through me. I tightened my scarf and cinched my belted peacoat to ward off the lingering chill.

Spring melt trailed along the curb beside me as I walked, leaking down the hill to where the river running through town would absorb it.

I paused as I approached the old stone church, gazing up on its beautiful exterior, loving the way its steeple stretched for the glory of the clouds without the pomp and circumstance of some other churches I'd seen.

"Pretty, right?" A woman was on her way up the hill, a Dalmatian straining against a leash in front of her.

I smiled and nodded, not taking my eyes off the bell tower. "Does the bell still ring every morning?" I asked.

"Oh yeah," she said. "Like clockwork. Night time

too. Preacher doesn't want us to forget dinner with our families. Get's this one in a tizzy every time," she indicated the dog. "She thinks it means I should be up and at 'em."

I laughed lightly. "Do you know what ever happened to the old Reverend?"

"There's been a fair few that have passed through here," she said. "Who you thinking of?"

"Greene?"

"Ah, that's going back a few years now. I don't think he ever did pastor again after leaving this church. Just slipped away rather quietly. Not sure what became of him. He'd be an old man now I suppose."

"In his 80's I'd think," I said.

"Hmm. Yes, that's about right. Bound to be someone around town who knows where he got to... or if he's still alive even... I don't mean..."

"It's all right," I assured her. "I know it's a possibility he could have passed by now... though I would love to look him up."

"Check in at the church office," the woman suggested. "They might know something. Should be open now I'd think. They leave the doors unlocked during the day. In case someone wants to pray."

"I might do that," I said, petting the head of the dog who nuzzled against me with her cold nose.

"Thank you."

I remained there for a moment as she walked away from me. I felt the tug of the old stone structure but couldn't bring myself to step into the street. *Not yet*, I thought. *I'm not ready yet.*

chapter two
guardian angels

I SAT ON THE RED VINYL BENCH IN THE booth by the window, biting my nails and staring across the street as I drummed my heel against the checkered tile. The town was quaint, the old store-fronts reeking of history and a stoic resistance to change.

There was only one other customer in the café—a man with huge, stained hands. I watched as he dumped three spoonfuls of sugar into his coffee before digging into a bowl of apple crisp, his eyes fixed on the waitress—a tiny wee thing with tired sneakers and a pretty face beneath untamed blond hair. She smiled at him every so often, a pained kind of upturned lip that seemed to linger closer to hurt than happiness. She didn't seem unhappy with him, just the world in general. Watching her made me sad. I wondered if she knew what a gift her cute little body was and how she needed to savour every moment of her youth before she found herself pushing forty and sitting in a café waiting for a ghost.

I wrapped my fingers around my coffee mug and willed myself to be calm.

I'd bought myself a new Moleskine notebook—it lay before me, open to its first page, white and virginal. I took my pen and wrote across the top: *Interview with Iris Carver*. I wasn't convinced she would actually come.

A BELL HUNG ABOVE THE DOOR FRAME, ringing its anthem anytime someone entered or left the café. It claimed attention like the church bell, but with less pomp and more friendliness. An older gentleman entered and I caught my breath as she whisked in behind him, slipping through before the door closed with another charming ding.

She wore layered skirts the colour of clouds. They swirled about her ankles as she spun around looking for me. Her sandals were leather and her toenails unpainted. Her eyes found mine and she let out a long breath, her smile warm, hands clasping the wooden beads around her neck. Her hair was wild and perfect, the sun catching little streaks of red and gold as she rushed over and slid into the booth across from me.

"You're here," I said, as if I didn't believe it.

"Of course," she answered, pushing her hair back and tugging out a little branch from among its tangles. She laughed and laid it on the table, pushing it towards me. "Always getting myself into some kind of trouble," she said.

I picked up the branch and turned it beneath my nose. It smelled of the forest.

"You're happy," I said.

"It's a beautiful day," she answered, pausing to look out the window where spring had nearly gained ownership over a particularly brutal winter.

The waitress approached us with a stainless steel carafe in her hand. "Can I warm it up for you?" she asked.

"Please," I said, pushing my mug towards the edge of the table, seeing her name tag on the front of her uniform. "Bird," I read, testing out the unusual name.

"Hmmhmm," she said.

"A bird in the hand is worth two in the bush," Iris said, giggling.

Bird didn't seem to hear her. "Someday I'll fly away," she said, rather wistfully.

"You don't like it here?" I asked.

She shrugged and pulled a cloth from her apron to wipe up a small dribble of coffee from the edge of the table. "There's better," she said. "Can I get you anything else?"

"Tea?" I asked, looking to Iris who nodded emphatically. "A cup of tea, please."

Bird frowned but nodded and left our table.

"What does that even mean?" I asked.

"What?" Iris said.

"The bird in the bush thing?"

"Oh," Iris said, waving her hand, her smile never drifting. "I don't know... like better to actually have something tangible—something you can really hold on to—than the idea of a lot of things you never actually touch."

"Hmmm," I said, nodding. "She seemed sad."

"There has always been sadness in this town," Iris said. "You have to learn to find the good or it will eat you alive."

"And your good was...?"

"My son, Joseph, of course."

"Of course."

"And Samuel." She looked out the window again and I followed her gaze, watching three robins rise from the sidewalk and fly across our field of vision. "He has the kind of softness to him that can forgive sin," she said.

The beautiful stain of that long ago love affair with Reverend Samuel Greene lingered upon her like blushing chiffon. It billowed around her, dyeing the air so she seemed wrapped in a pale pink light.

Bird returned with a cup and saucer and a little silver teapot, steam pouring from the spout. She cast a questioning look my way and I nodded to the opposite side of the table. She set it down in front of Iris. "You expecting someone else?" she asked me.

"Just us. Thank you, Bird."

She raised an eyebrow, but left without asking more questions.

"The nest of the blind bird is made by God," Iris said.

"What do you mean?" I asked.

"People get lost in this town if they don't find something to cling to. No one is invisible. God is watching. She's got an army around her, that one."

My eyes followed Bird back to the kitchen, seeing nothing following her but her own shadow. "And what of me?" I asked. "Do I have an army?"

"You don't need an army, friend. You have a champion though, right over there." She pointed to an empty table across the diner and gave a little wave. "You're never alone. He's got your back."

Goosebumps raised on my neck and I pulled my cardigan tighter around my shoulders.

"Does that make you uncomfortable?" she asked. "The idea of a guardian angel?"

I tapped my fingers against my mug and thought for a moment. "A little," I finally said. "I mean... I've never really thought about it, I guess. You think he's always there?"

"Always," she said.

I squirmed in my seat. "Why couldn't I have a woman guardian?"

Iris giggled, delighted by my awkwardness. "He's not a man or a woman, silly, he's an angel... I'm not sure he takes great pleasure in watching you shower. That being said, I'm not sure he dislikes it either." Her grin was playful and I couldn't help but smile back at her. "I will say this though," she said, leaning forward, "he's quite handsome."

"Like Samuel?"

Her eyes took on the shiny quality of one lost in a memory and a small hint of rose bloomed on her cheeks. "You've met him then?" she said.

"Samuel? No. Not really. Not *three-dimensionally*."

Iris crinkled her nose and tilted her head. "Right," she said. "He has a bit of magic about him."

"I think he would say the same of you."

She giggled and pulled her feet up on the vinyl bench. "Kissing him is like finding forever. Have you felt that? Have you felt forever?"

I struggled to find a moment in my own history that could capture a piece of what she described. "Maybe," I said. "Like losing yourself without missing yourself."

She grinned and shook her head. "That doesn't make any sense."

"Like finding yourself."

"Ah," she said. "That's it. You *do* know."

"I like to think that I do. What else is there if we don't?"

She nodded like I'd stumbled upon the profound. "He's beyond me now," she said.

"What do you mean?"

"Just past my fingertips. Just beyond my reach. He was just here, you know? I still smell him on my skin. When I close my eyes I feel him beside me, and when I listen hard I hear him calling my name." She brought her hand up beneath her nose and closed her eyes, breathing in the bit of him that clung to her.

"How long have you been looking for him?"

She shrugged. "Forever? A minute? I think I've forgotten how to understand time."

"How did you know what time to meet me?"

"Huh." She leaned back in her seat, drumming her fingertips on the tabletop. Her action made no sound, but caused a slight vibration I could feel through the table where my own arms were resting. "I don't know that I did," she said. "Time is different when you're lost than when you are found."

"And which are you?" I asked.

"I am neither lost nor found. I just am. Like a circle. Round and round. Always here but never here. I always hear but am never heard."

"I hear you."

"Are you sure?" She leaned forward, moving her face into the steam pouring from the mouth of the teapot so that her image seemed to shift and morph. I thought again about the silent vibration of her fingers.

I nursed my coffee and studied her face before answering deliberately. "Yes. I'm sure."

"Of course you are," she said, sitting back again. "I'm yours as much as I belong to myself."

"Have you always spoken in riddles?"

"Perhaps. Have you always been drawn to characters who are grotesquely flawed?"

I grinned. "Perhaps."

"Like him?" She nodded towards the man sitting with his back to us.

I studied him and felt his story, filing away the

weight of his spirit as it stirred the warm café air.

"Which is worse," Iris said, "the sinner or the sin?"

I looked from her back to the man again. "What has he done?"

"You know more than you're telling me," she said.

I felt a tingling in my fingertips. "Even terrible things can be done out of pure intentions."

"But terrible things done out of pain are still terrible things, even if intentions are pure."

"Is there anything unforgivable?"

"Yes. But only a few things."

My cup was empty again and I shifted in my seat. "How do you feel about the things done to you?" I asked.

"Fair," she said.

"That's a poor answer."

"Is it?" She folded her hands into a peak and held her fingertips at her chin. "Bad things were done to me. You know this. I, in turn, did wrong to another... and to myself. My suffering bookended my poor choices. That's fair. The order in which a thing occurs doesn't matter. What matters is that the universe is just. One good turn deserves another."

chapter three
by any other name

MOVEMENT BEHIND THE COUNTER distracted Iris as a new waitress pushed through the swinging kitchen doors.

"Rose?" Iris gasped as she spoke the name, sliding from the booth and standing beside the table, eyes frozen on the red-headed girl as she wiped down the counter. "Rose!" But the girl didn't look our way until I lifted my coffee mug, indicating I'd like a refill. She shot me a warm smile and left her cloth on the counter as she grabbed the coffee pot. Iris remained paralyzed beside our table.

"Rose?" I asked, as the girl poured my coffee.

"Pardon?"

"Sorry," I said. "Is your name Rose?" An intense sense of recognition overwhelmed me as I looked on her face.

"Nope," she said. "Rose is my grandmother. I'm Likely."

"Likely?"

"Yup. *Likely* to pour you a great cup of coffee." She beamed at her own joke as she filled my cup and I smiled, though I was shaken by Iris' still form, standing so rigidly and disturbed beside the girl.

"I'm sorry," Likely said. "Do you know my grandmother? People say I look like her."

"Spitting image," Iris whispered.

"I don't know her," I said. "Just a bit of her story."

"Oh yeah, since that interview a few years back she's become a bit of a legend around here. Most of the other women wouldn't talk. Too painful, I guess. Grandma is a firecracker though, and once she learned that Roth was dead she kind of got over it and needed people to know what happened."

"Roth is dead?" Iris slid back into the booth, resting her hands flat on the tabletop as if to steady herself.

"Anyway," Likely said, "need anything else right now?"

"No. Thanks."

"Roth is dead?" Iris repeated as Likely left the table.

I rustled through my bag and pulled out a faded newspaper clipping. I flattened it on the table and turned it around, sliding it across so she could read it.

HARRIDAN BLUFFS PROPHET, DEAD AT HANDS OF OWN SON

John Peter Roth was rushed to hospital with severe head trauma after suffering an assault by one Peter Callum. He succumbed to his wounds late last night.

Convicted of multiple counts of the sexual abuse of a minor, following the scandalous outing and raid of the Harridan Bluffs Commune in October of 1961, Roth was remanded to protective custody for fear that inmates would not allow a safe existence within the general population. Though serving a life-sentence, with no record of conflict and without contest, he met requirements for an early release.

At the age of 72, Roth was released on parole, sent to live in a half-way house, and required to work a part-time minimum wage job as a dishwasher in a nearby restaurant.

On his second day at the job, Callum accosted Roth in the kitchen of 3rd Street Diner.

Callum, one of Roth's many children sired during his time as the self-proclaimed prophet of Harridan Bluffs, is in police custody, held on second degree murder charges, awaiting trial. He could not post bail.

I WATCHED IRIS' FACE AS SHE READ THE article, shocked to see the pained way she held her mouth. I didn't expect her to grieve the death of the man who forced her into marriage when she was only twelve years old. I slid my hand across the table until it almost touched hers. "He didn't suffer," I told her. "From what I know, it was one quick hit to the head.

He never regained consciousness."

Iris shook her head. "Not him," she said. "I feel no sorrow for that monster." She let her finger fall below the name of the man who had attacked him. "Him. That's my brother."

"I'm sorry," I said, ashamed by my oversight. "I hadn't realized." I retrieved the paper and stuck it back in my bag. "If it makes you feel better, the jury had little sympathy for Roth and that was reflected in the short sentence Peter received. Here. Wait a second." I pulled out my phone and did a quick search. Slipping out of my seat, I moved around the booth so we could sit side by side. "This was his statement after the sentencing," I said, holding out the phone so she could watch the small screen.

A man in his fifties, thinning hair and eyes that blinked too often, stood on the steps outside a court-house, a lawyer on his left while he spoke into a cluster of microphones. "I know I've done something that, in the eyes of the law and God, is not right, and I accept the punishment assigned me. But I will not now, nor will I ever, feel regret for ridding the world of a man as cruel and indecent as John Peter Roth. He destroyed everything he touched, and never once did he fulfill the role of father in my upbringing. I *will* do my time and I *will* sleep well at night. In fact, I'm sleeping better now than I have since the initial raid back in '61."

I tapped pause on the video and Iris ran her finger over the face of her brother. "He's so old."

I laughed and tucked my phone back in my pocket.

"I haven't seen him since he was a little boy. Since before I ran away. He was the only child my mother bore while we were part of the Harridan Bluffs community." She touched her own face. "Am *I* old?"

I shook my head and studied her so closely I should have felt embarrassed. Not a crease on her smooth face. "You're perfect," I said.

She laughed. "Sometimes I feel ancient. Other times I feel brand new."

"That's part of your magic," I said.

She smiled and it lit a fresh spark of happiness in her eyes.

"Oh good," I said. "I thought I'd wrecked everything."

"The truth never wrecks, it only educates. I'm pleased to know the truth, but I'm sad about my brother." She looked off to where Likely was brewing a fresh pot of coffee. "And I miss my friend."

"Rose?"

She nodded. "She really does look like her. Has her spunk too. Heritage is how people live forever."

I smiled at that, thinking of my own children, little pieces of me.

My third coffee empty, I excused myself from the table.

I RETURNED FROM THE RESTROOM TO SEE our booth sitting empty. Scanning the restaurant, I found Iris sitting at a table, opposite the man with the huge hands and the apple crisp. She stared at him intently, a look of desperate softness painted on her face. I held my breath as she reached across the table and rested her small hands over his. He didn't move or acknowledge her presence and she wasn't disturbed by his rudeness.

"My late husband had a dog named Wolf when he was growing up," she said, her whisper eating up the air in the restaurant, making everything warm and sleepy as she breathed a piece of story at this stranger who pushed his morning dessert around a puddle of melted ice cream without looking at her.

"Wolf was a bird dog," she continued. "Paisley'd take him hunting. The thing about a bird dog is, they fetch the duck or partridge after it's been shot down, but even though their jaws are strong as death, they carry that poor bird as gentle as a mother with her newborn so as not to bruise the meat. You've got a bit of Wolf in you. I see it there, waiting for you to realize you don't need to bite down so hard."

I watched as a fat tear bloomed from her left eye and spilled down her cheek. "You'll find it," she whispered, her words floating across the table. He sucked in his breath as if the world suddenly came into focus, and saw me standing there, staring.

"Can I help you?" he asked, his voice rough with a heaviness that spoke through his eyes, the revelation of an Irish accent in the shape of his vowels.

"Sorry." I gave Iris a *'come on'* look, but she lingered a moment longer before wiping the tear from her cheek and gently resting those tear-dampened fingers on the man's shoulder as she passed him on her way back to me.

"What were you doing?" I asked. "Do you know that man?"

"We're all part of the same thing. If we're willing to touch each other's brokenness, we're able to heal. Do you believe in miracles?"

I longed for a magnifying glass. I wanted to study her. I wanted to catch her in a jar, like a child fascinated by a firefly, and watch her glow. "I believe in you," I whispered.

She thought this was hilarious, and laughter bubbled from her in such a way that it shook the air around us. "Why did you want to meet with me?" she asked, the echo of her laughter lingering in the cadence of her question.

"Are you not happy to be here?"

"Oh yes. Very much. But I worry you're looking for something I can't give you."

"I only want to be close to you for a little while. To know you better. To be in your story. Part of it. More than its narrator."

She pointed to my notebook, still open on the table. "You've written nothing down."

I tapped my temple with my finger and placed my other hand over my heart. "Yes I have."

Her smile was sweet as she tossed her hair and moved towards the exit. "I'd like to go to my clearing now," she said.

I threw a bill on the table and held the door open for her as we left, leaving behind her untouched pot of tea, no longer steaming.

chapter four
into the woods

I DIDN'T QUESTION IRIS WHEN SHE WALKED past the entrance to the old Carver driveway, journeying farther down the road to where the unused railroad cut across. It made sense, her not wanting to see the house—that place where she made so many mistakes, where she'd taken lovers to pay the bills. And though it was the place she eventually fell in love, it would always be four walls of sadness. Sometimes, no matter the good that follows, the shadow of a past hurt can dominate what should be a place of peace.

Stepping off the road onto the rusty tracks brought an eerie foreboding as bare branches formed a natural canopy, cutting off some of the sun.

"I've never come this way before," Iris said, balancing along one of the rails, her arms out to steady herself.

"Why not?"

"Never needed to. There was a path right by the house." She tucked a strand of hair behind her ear and jumped to the opposite rail to continue her balancing act. "Who do you suppose lives there now?"

"I don't know."

"Do you think Paisley's old truck is still there?" Her late husband's rusty truck had taken up residence in her yard. Too beat up to drive and tires too rotten to move, she'd grown a herb garden in the truck bed as a tribute to his memory.

"We could go see if you like," I offered.

She shook her head. "I wouldn't want to impose."

"You wouldn't like to visit your old home?" I asked. I didn't remind her the clearing was also on private property.

"Home is just a point of view," she said, pointing her toe with each step as she moved with the grace of a dancer. "Kids came down here every year." She spun on the rail, her skirts twirling around her bare legs, her voice close then far as her projection spun with her. "They liked to tell my story around a campfire. Not the whole story. Just the parts that made me sound like a wicked woman. A witch."

"I remember." It was one of the first scenes I'd written, long before I uncovered the soft edges of her character—a tenderness untouched by local folklore.

"Such a strange tradition." She moved forward again, her skirts unaware the body they graced no longer spun. "Do you think they still do it?"

"The kids?" I asked. "It would surprise me if they didn't."

"I hope they do," she said. "Even if they get the story wrong, it's nice if people remember Paisley. Is that strange or morbid of me?"

I paused, pursing my lips before answering. "Yes."

She laughed and jumped off the rail to follow a footpath into the forest. "Yeah, I guess it is. But there's something very romantic about becoming a legend, isn't there?"

I agreed, but I didn't say so. I didn't want to say out loud there could be any romance to a man's suicide. Especially when his reasoning had much to do with Iris' choices. Paisley had been a simple man, but he had been kind. I knew in my heart, when Iris married him after escaping her life at Harridan Bluffs, she had no intention of hurting him. Past pains clouded her judgement.

When a pregnancy brought twins, and she was too broken to consider raising a daughter, it broke Paisley to discover she had thrown the baby away. He died long before that daughter came back. If he had only hung on, instead of finding solace at the end of a rope, he might have known a true happily ever after.

"IT'S CHANGED," SHE SAID AS WE STEPPED from beneath the trees into a little clearing in the middle of the Carver land.

"Has it?"

She turned a slow circle and her skirts belled out in a parade of white eyelet springtime. "The stones are gone. They once stood right here." She passed her hand, palm down, over the smooth dirt floor, scattered with the remnants of branches knocked down in winter storms. Her stones, twelve dark soldiers, had once rested in a circle in the centre of the clearing. She had claimed the space within them as her sanctuary, her own church in the wildwood.

I closed my eyes and raised my face to the open arms of the trees surrounding us, feeling the kiss of the sun where it broke through the greenery— enough to shed bits of light and dapple the ground with little touches of warmth.

"*Ring out the old, ring in the new; ring happy bells, across the snow...*"

I opened my eyes to find she had vanished and I spun round, searching. She carried through the verses of her favourite song and a sob built up within my chest as the lyrics splashed over me. More was said in the pregnant pauses between phrases than could ever be articulated in those words penned long ago. Every sacred Sunday she'd spent beneath these trees had included those words. They were as much a part of her story as her wistful eyes and shadowed upbringing. "Where are you?" I called.

"Looking for Paisley's footprints," she replied.

I turned back around to find her standing in the high crook of the old oak, where long ago, her husband had lost his life. Her sandals lay on the ground at the base of the tree.

"Do you think he was frightened?" she asked.

"Of course," I replied.

"Yes. I think so too. I wish he hadn't been. I wish he'd been brave. Though I think a brave man would face his pain rather than hang it all on a rope." She took a step out from the trunk, toes curling over the edge of the thick branch, arms out to steady her as she took another step. I waited for the branch to bend but it didn't even creak.

"Be careful," I called.

She laughed. It sounded like crying. "Was Paisley careful?"

"Only careful people get the job done."

She scoffed and whipped her head back, flinging loose hair from her face. She crouched at the place on the branch still bearing the scar of the rope that had once swung with such self-loathing violence. "You have to be awfully occupied with yourself to do a thing like that," she quoted.

"Hemingway?"

"*For Whom The Bell Tolls* was his scripture."

"I remember."

Being in this place caused a shift in her. No longer the playful spirit from the diner, in this clearing she became an introspective soul. She lowered herself to the branch, sitting so her skirts hung like a queen riding side-saddle. She swung her bare feet, stirring the air with whatever magic came with her. "I brought Samuel here once," she said, her voice distant, like it had drifted off to catch the memory.

I backed up against a tree on the opposite side of the clearing and slid down its trunk so I was sitting on the cold forest floor. My breath shot out before me and I hugged my knees against my chest, tucking my fingers into the pockets created at their bend, trying to keep warm.

"Do you know him?" she asked, as if she'd forgotten our earlier conversation. "Samuel?"

"As much as he revealed to me when I first told

his story."

She nodded, a small smile the only makeup she'd ever need. "You know him. He changes a person, you know? Softens them somehow. He takes hard things and makes them pliable. He takes secrets and makes them atoneable." Her face fell. "Do you know where he is? I've been looking for him for so long now. I fear the change he made in me will shift if I don't find myself close to him again."

I remained silent, clinging to a truth I wasn't yet ready to part with.

"Paisley was my hero," she said. "He saved me from a life of slavery and abuse. But Samuel was my salvation. He saved me from myself."

"That's beautiful," I said. "You're lucky."

She laughed but it seemed void of heart. "Am I? There is no luck in loneliness. Do you know where he is?" she asked again. "Are you not telling me because the truth would hurt me?"

"I don't know where he is."

"Would knowing break my heart?"

I remained silent. The poor thing. As innocent and broken as she had been those many years ago when she'd escaped her oppressed existence.

"I think I might be made of glass," she said. "I think a broken heart would mean I'd shatter into shining shards, vast enough to cover the earth.

Artists might make stained-glass of my heart.

"I once decorated this forest with wind-chimes made from pieces of glass, you know. Do you think perhaps those pieces were the shards of another heart? Do you think the songs of the chimes were the songs of heartbreak?" She gazed off into the trees.

"No," she answered herself. "They sang songs of worship. And worship is not heartbreak. Worship is the purest form of love... so don't tell me. I don't want to know where he is. He'll find me when heaven deems it fit. I do wonder though... what became of my wind-chimes?"

"I could show you if you like," I offered.

"Will it hurt me?"

"Only so much as love hurts."

"Ah... but love hurts most of all, doesn't it?"

"Sometimes."

"You know this?"

"I do."

"I can tell. I see through your stoic exterior. You're soft inside. You might be a little like me. Though without the scarring, I hope."

"We all bear the scars of past hurt."

"Oh, of course. Within." She pulled at her skirts, piling them up against her stomach so her legs hung bare, her pale flesh bright like its own sunshine. Even from my seat on the forest floor I could see the puckered skin on her thigh, the rude etching of a letter 'R'.

"Only the most unfortunate are cursed to roam this mortal coil, damaged without," she said.

With her head bent to examine the scar, I could no longer see her face. The forest grew a little darker because of it. Her hair formed a long veil, protecting her pain from my gaze. I leaned back against the tree, fighting a pressure in my own chest that made me want to dig into the soil to find something colder than the air to ease the swelling of a painful memory.

She traced the scar with a slender finger. "You've heard it said that one of the mechanisms of our psyche is the mind's ability to forget pain?"

"Yes."

"Like in childbirth. What is more violent than childbirth?"

I remained silent.

"Yet the moment that child is in your arms, the pain backs away like retreating fog across a morning field. Do you know the feeling of a blade across your skin?"

I shook my head, and though she didn't look my way I knew she sensed my motion in the way a bird feels a storm long before the first drop of rain.

"It doesn't hurt at first. The fear hurts more than the blade. There is pressure and panic but there is no real pain until you see the blood across the bedsheets."

I wanted her to stop but I'd lost my words.

I knew her story, but as that of an outsider. A passive observer. I didn't want the intimate details. I wanted the shroud of my chosen ignorance. *Don't. Don't. Don't.* And yet, what therapy could there be for her if the one person with ears to hear chose to fill those ears with dirt rather than let her spill her truth like breadcrumbs. At twelve years old she'd been forced into a cult marriage with a monster. *Twelve years old.* My stomach turned.

"What can a child do against a man?" she asked. "I'd stolen the knife, thinking myself some storybook heroine. I was nothing but a juvenile fool. He'd laid me on the bed. He was actually gentle. If I'd just let him... it wouldn't have been so bad. Inevitable anyway. But I reached into my pocket and pulled out that knife.

"Have you watched a man's eyes go from lust to rage? It's a subtle shift. The two seem closely entwined somehow. There is no weapon more terrifying than that. He grabbed my wrist. He squeezed until my bones bruised and I dropped the blade. Then he sat on me. Backwards. Full weight on my chest as he ripped up that white wedding smock they made me wear. I cried while he cut me and he told me that I would never again try to defy him. He was marking me for him. Claiming me. I didn't know the damage until he lifted his weight off me and stood back beside the bed to admire his art. I sat up, looking down to see what he had done, watching the blood leak down my thigh onto the bed. When the pain of it finally registered, it was like hot fire. My heartbeat was in my leg and every pulse brought me closer to full panic. When I tried to scream, he pushed me back again, hand over my mouth as he used his other to undo his pants."

I had buried my head against my knees, shaking it back and forth to rid myself of the images she painted, knowing I was to blame somehow.

"There is some pain you never forget," she said.

I looked up to find her squatting in front of me.

"He put his name on me. I have to carry that with me everywhere. When you give birth, the child is your scar. But you love it. You embrace it. You thrill to have the burden. When the prophet of Harridan Bluffs carves himself into your flesh there's no happy coo to bring you back from that darkness. There are distractions, yes. And other love stories. But this will always be a part of me. Scars are unshakable. It is in their very nature."

"How do you carry on?" I asked.

"When the world won't let you go, you learn to

carve your own path opposite the carving forced on you. You never forget. Never. But you learn to find solace in softer things. Paisley. Samuel. Joseph. Good things that don't mould." She stood, still barefoot, an early spring flower. "I'd like to see my wind-chimes now."

I wiped a tear from my cheek and took a trembling breath.

"You cry for me?" she asked.

"I'm so sorry," I said.

"Sorry doesn't mend a thing. Sorry is a word without action. I don't ask for your sorrow. I ask for your friendship."

"You have it. You've always had it."

"Good. Thank you." She held out her hand to help me stand, but I raised myself without her assistance, feeling unworthy of her touch after the darkness she just shared.

"Are you happy, Iris?"

She tilted her head back, her hair falling down her back in cascades of red and gold. "Happy?"

"Yes."

The sun through the branches decorated her face with a lovely mixture of light and shadow. "I might be," she said. "In as much as anybody is. I've learned to be exactly who I am in the midst of twilight doings. I am an overcomer. I am proud of that. And yes,

I know happiness. Of a sort. Are you? Happy, I mean."

"Usually."

"Good. My wind-chimes?"

"Right. This way."

chapter five
rest in peace

"HE TOLD ME HE WOULD BUILD ME A church," she said as we turned our attention from the forest to the weather-beaten logs on what was once the old Carver hunting cabin. "I thought it was the daydream of a silly boy. But he was so insistent. I didn't understand why he needed it." She took a step back to get a good look at the peak where a square bell tower broke through. One slat of wood had come loose and hung askew, but the rest of the structure seemed to be intact. "It does have the look of a church, doesn't it?"

"It does."

"Can we go inside?"

"I think he would want that."

I led the way up on the wooden stoop. It groaned beneath my weight, one board almost rotted through. I took a wide step to land on the edge of the door-frame and put my hand on the metal handle, pushing the door open.

"Wait!" Iris said, stepping up beside me and reaching to the right where, on the outer wall, be-yond the edge of the porch, there was a small wooden plaque with the letters of her name burned into the wood. She ran her fingers through the groove of the 'R'—just like the scar on her thigh.

"Look," I said, pointing to the flowerbed where the barkish roots of an iris plant were visible beneath a scattering of dead leaves. "And there," I pointed farther down the wall where another plaque said 'Rose'. We followed the beds around the building, all labelled for their flower.

When we returned to the front, Iris sat on the ground, white skirts spilling out around her, undis-turbed by the dirt.

"What is it?" I asked.

Her eyes were wet when they met mine. "It's The Promise Book," she said.

"What?"

"The Promise Book. From Harridan Bluffs. On her tenth birthday, every Harridan girl was placed in

The Promise Book. It was from there they were chosen to be child brides."

I knelt down in front of her. "I'm sorry," I said. I remembered the story.

"We were all named for flowers. Every one of us. The Prophet told us to bloom where we were planted so that when we were properly ripened we might be plucked."

"But you weren't born at Harridan Bluffs."

"No, but the universe knew I'd end up there." She gestured to the wall. "They're here. They're all here. Rose, Daisy, Zinnia, Lily, Aster... all of them. He took them back. Joseph took them back." A smile split her face and she tipped it back to catch the sun even as a tear slipped down her cheek. "He took them all back. Good boy, Joseph. Good boy!" She hopped up from the ground, dress unmarred, and skipped back to the porch, squeezing past the heavy door I'd propped open, waving at me to follow.

IT SMELLED LIKE SUMMER CAMP INSIDE—THE damp woodsy musk you hate in your own home but embrace when it is somewhere wild. The floors were clean of dirt and the walls and rafters clear of dust and cobwebs. A table and two chairs stood to the left of the door, a brown jacket hanging over one of the chairs. A metal speckled cup and a spoon sat on the table. A small countertop housed a large refillable water dispenser, a mason jar full of tea bags, three more metal cups, and a stack of paperbacks. Four hand-built pews sat facing the wall beneath the loft. A small wood stove perched in the centre of the same wall, a kettle sitting atop it with steam escaping from the spout, a silver urn the only decoration on a shelf beside the fire. A chimney carried heat into the loft where it vented out the east side. A neat pile of wood stood against the south wall.

Iris gasped when she turned to her right and saw the window. "Oh, it's so pretty!" She approached it slowly and ran her fingers over the glass—her wind-chime pieces. "Joseph made this?"

"Your daughter made it," I told her.

"My daughter made it?"

"Yes. Grace."

"Grace?" She stumbled back, knocking her legs into a pew where she sat to stare at it. "My daughter?"

"Yes."

"Joseph found her?"

"He did." I sat in the pew ahead of her, turned so we were face to face.

"He followed his heart?"

"I guess he did."

"And they were a family?" she asked.

"I like to think so."

"Oh..." the sound escaped her lips like a sigh. "That is good news. What do you think she thinks of me?"

"Some questions are better left unasked."

She nodded slowly. "Yes. You're right. Of course, you're right." She rose from her seat, moving like she was in a dream. She climbed the ladder to the loft overhead where a large wind-chime hung like a chandelier from the centre of the bell-tower.

I joined her in the loft and plucked the rusty nail out of the air that hung from the end of the clapper. "Do you remember?" I asked her.

She held out her hand, turning it over so her palm faced up. A faint scar seemed to glow from her smooth skin. "It pierced me here," she said softly, as if she hadn't thought of that moment for a very long time. "Joseph had pulled it from his wall... I'd fallen and it went into my hand..."

I let the nail fall so the chimes rang out. Iris closed her eyes and let the sound wash over her.

"Grace used the rest of your wind-chime pieces to build this for Joseph. For you."

She didn't move until the last little tinkle faded into the vaulted wood ceiling. The nail continued to sway but we could read the word etched on it. "Don't make a relic of me," she whispered, her eyes wet as the truth descended on her. "Am I real?"

"Of course."

"I'm not here."

"But you are."

"Who put the kettle on?"

Her abrupt change of focus caused me to pause and shake my head as I caught up with her train of thought. I'd been so absorbed in her presence I'd ignored all the signs of life around us. For the first time since entering the cabin, it occurred to me that someone must have only just stepped away before we got there. "I don't know," I told her.

She was backing into a corner. "Is it Joseph?" she asked.

On the floor below, I heard boots stomp as someone came inside. Iris crept up to the railing, her eyes going wide, her hands clamped over her mouth as she backed up again.

"Hello?" he called. "Someone here?"

"Hi," I said over the railing. "Hi. Sorry. The door was unlocked and I used to know this place... Sorry."

He was older than me, hair nearing grey, quite handsome in an old western kind of way. He studied me, his brow furrowed like he thought he might know me. He ran a hand over his face, bringing his fingers together at his chin as he did a quick sweep of the cabin for other intruders. Behind me, Iris whimpered.

His face softened from concern into a smile and he finally dropped his hand and kicked off his boots. "Did you get dragged out here as a kid to hear ghost stories in the woods?"

"Something like that," I said, immediately drawn to him.

Behind me, Iris was shaking her head. "No, no, no, no, no," she repeated. "Can't be. Can't be Joseph." Her pitch grew higher and higher until she finally peeled herself away from the wall, raced down the ladder, and out of the cabin. Her escape caused the wind-chime to give a little clink as her movement shifted the air.

"Everything okay?" he asked, his glance going to the door as if he'd seen something out of the corner of his eye, before returning to me.

I climbed down the ladder and introduced myself, shaking his hand. "So you're Joseph Carver."

"One and the same." He lifted the kettle from the stove and poured himself a cup, adding a tea bag to the steaming mug. He offered me one as well but I shook my head. "What brings you here?" he asked, sitting at the table and inviting me to do the same.

"Memories," I said. A magnetic energy made me want to pull my chair closer and explore his face like a sculptor might touch their own creation. As a child, when I couldn't sleep, my mother would run her finger over my nose, my chin, my eyelids. I wanted to do the same to him and I squirmed in my seat, fighting the urge as I kept my hands planted in my lap. "Why do *you* come here?" I asked.

"The same reason, I suppose. I don't come out here as much as I used to, but it's good to remember where you came from."

"Your mother..."

"Yes. Funny thing about time... I feel like it was only yesterday... but then, other times, I feel like she was never here, like I dreamed it all."

"You still live at the house?"

"Oh yes. And my sister still tends the garden there—she doesn't have room for one at her place in town."

"Grace?"

"Of course. Once in a while she brings the kids along with her, but they're older now, you know. Not as much fun to hang out on the farm as when they were little."

"The kids?"

"My nephews and nieces."

"Right. So you never had children of your own?"

"'Course I did. Every student I've ever taught was like my own child." He shook his head a little sadly. "We wanted children but the doctors advised against it with Margaret's M.S. She's still doing good though. Haven't had to move the bedroom downstairs yet. She doesn't make the trek out here with me anymore. This place doesn't mean the same to her though that it does to me." He took a long drink of his tea and looked around the cabin. "I don't know what it is. I feel Momma here a little stronger today than usual. You knew her?"

"Yes."

"You must have brought a little bit of her with you." He squinted as he studied my face. "You would have been quite young when you knew her. I don't remember other kids being around... except the kids that met here in the forest on the summer solstice."

"Everyone has their secrets," I said.

He leaned back in his chair, holding his mug in cupped hands. "Isn't that right. You sure you don't want a tea?"

"No. Thank you," I said. "I should really get going. I've imposed long enough."

"So few people knew her. It's nice to talk to someone who did."

"What about Samuel?" I asked.

"Samuel Greene?"

"Yes."

"Oh, he passed a few years back. Never did love another woman like he did Momma."

Overwhelming sadness put pressure against my chest and I took a shaky breath before replying. "What a waste."

Joseph shook his head. "He wouldn't say so. He'd say that he'd had his great love and many aren't so fortunate."

"So you kept in touch?"

"Over the years. We'd see each other on occasion. Grace invited him to Easter and Christmas dinners up until he was too weak with the cancer to leave his room. He never stopped loving her, you know."

"There is no end to great love, is there?"

"Suppose not."

I'd inched my way to the door by then, and said my goodbyes, trying to be gracious. I felt warmed by his calming nature, but found it strange how quickly he had welcomed me, a trespasser, to sit at his table.

IRIS' VOICE FLOATED TO ME FROM THE LEFT as I stepped out onto the rotted porch. "I thought I should be planted where he put me." She was sitting beneath the 'Iris' sign, cross-legged on the roots of the iris bulbs. "Was it really him?" she asked.

I walked off the porch and turned to face her. She looked even younger now, a little more broken and beautiful in the way an old porcelain doll is beautiful. Fragile and precious. "It was. Why didn't you want to see him?" I asked.

"He's not mine anymore. Our memories are enough. It would hurt him to see me. Do you think he's happy?"

"He's made a good life for himself."

"I'm glad."

"You're a grandmother."

She nodded, slow tears moving down her cheeks. "I heard. The door wasn't closed."

"How do you feel?" I asked.

"I remember being happy. I remember being in love. That should be enough to let go, shouldn't it?"

"What are you hanging onto?"

"I don't want it to be over."

"Was Samuel your great love?"

"Our time was so short."

"All our time is short."

"But ours was shorter than most. I'm afraid to truly close my eyes. I'm afraid that if I do, when I open them, he won't be there. That would be hell."

"There's no room for someone like you in hell."

"Are you sure?"

I held out my hand to her but she stood without my assistance. "I've lost my shoes," she said.

"Do you really need them where you're going?"

"No," she whispered.

WE WALKED SLOWLY AS WE RETRACED OUR steps along the railway. Iris began singing her 'Ring Out The Bells' song before we'd even stepped out of the woods. Her haunting voice caused the hairs on my arms to stand on end. When it began to fade, I turned to see her stopped and looking back towards the forest from which we'd come.

"Iris?"

"I think this is where you leave me," she said.

I walked back, passing her so I could look into her face. "I don't want to leave you."

She sat down, right where she stood. Her bare feet stuck out from under her skirts and though my breath shot out ahead of me in billowing grey clouds, no air moved by her mouth. "Why did you come here?" she asked.

I sat in front of her, crossing my legs and leaning forward. "I just had so many questions," I told her.

"Was I here before you came?" For a moment I thought she might be mocking me, but then I realized she genuinely didn't know.

"I don't know, Iris. What do you remember?"

"Everything is a circle," she said. "A lot of time has passed. But no time has passed. I remember falling asleep in Samuel's arms. He smelled like soap and green tea. That is the last time I saw him. I drifted. I floated. I was wrapped up in softness.

Sometimes I felt the echo of his voice, but I think I was alone. No light. No darkness either. Just an emptiness that wasn't quite lonely. I slept. I dreamed. Are you sure I'm real?"

"As real as anything I've ever known."

"Am I *your* great love?"

I laughed even though I knew she was being serious. "Maybe you are, in a way."

She nodded and a smile split through her brokenness. "I like that," she said. "I'm happy to be your great love. Though you must understand that you are not mine."

"I know," I said, already feeling the loss of her leaving.

"Can *you* let go?" she asked.

"It's my fault you are here."

"I know. So can you? Let go?"

"Samuel is waiting?" I wondered. "Has my need to keep you close prevented him from finding you where he is?"

"There's only one way to find out, isn't there?"

"Will you let me know?"

"Love always finds a way. It is the touching of two souls. When something is real, it can't be denied. Not through time or distance or the selfishness of another."

Her accusation stung and my eyes burned as I

settled myself into the truth of her words.

She leaned forward and pressed her lips against my forehead. I felt little more than a cool whisper of air, but it was enough to know she forgave me, though I knew I didn't deserve it.

"Sing with me?" She began the first verse of her song again, and I joined her, not letting my eyes drift from her face, my voice breaking as it weaved together with hers.

> *Ring out, wild bells, to the wild sky*
> *The flying cloud, the frosty light:*
> *The year is dying in the night*
> *Ring out, wild bells, and let him die.*

She faded as we sang. I squinted and focused in an effort to hang on to her, but she disappeared from my vision before the final words left my lips. "Ring out, wild bells, and let *her fly*," I said to the loneliness in front of me.

I sat there for a length of time unbeknownst to me. The cold ground had worked its icy fingers into my bones when, from across the long path and roadway towards town, came the sound of peeling bells, stumbling their chime from the church set high on the hill, that church where Samuel Greene once mourned the loss of that same precious bell, and then his one great love, Iris Carver.

I picked myself up from the ground, brushed the dirt from my clothes, and began a purposeful march back towards town, thinking I could still smell her on the air, though she was nowhere to be found.

chapter six
here is the church

THE CHURCH DOOR CREAKED AS I PUSHED it open. Loathe to make a mess on the clean wooden floor, I slipped out of my wet boots and left them beneath the coat rack in the small foyer before stepping into the sanctuary. The high ceiling rose above me, pointing its way to heaven as I slid into the back pew. I let the holy hush of the place wash over me as I sat and soaked in the presence of its history. The massive organ pipes rose up to the ceiling on the left and the stained-glass shepherd watched me from the large central window as I stared back at him.

"Hello?" I whispered into the stillness, my breath causing motes of dust to dance through coloured evening rays beaming down through a side window. I closed my eyes and captured the scent of the place: the wood and wax and sins atoned. If I listened carefully I could find the echo of Reverend Greene's voice pulsing off the walls, the tender sincerity with which he preached his heart to the people who filled these seats on Sunday mornings long ago. His absence felt unjust and I missed him with a raw regret that surprised me in its potency.

When the sun diminished to nothing but a dull orange light leaking through the window, I slipped from the sanctuary as quietly as I'd entered and followed the hallway to where a narrow set of stairs led towards the belfry. Following the path of one before me, I left the stairs and hoisted myself between studs until I shimmied my body all the way to the ledge surrounding the little church bell. I groaned as my limbs protested the vigour meant for a much younger set of legs.

Through the slats of the open window I could feel the cool air, still edged with memories of winter, whispering through in gentle breaths to cool my skin, hot from the climb.

By pressing my face against the slats I could see the whole town in the fading light. It was charming; evergreen branches filling planters along the bridge, children throwing rocks in the river, a school yard that still allowed a jungle gym. The streetlights flickered on as I memorized the scene.

Here is the church, here is the steeple, look out the tower and see all the people. I smiled to myself and swallowed a burst of sadness that threatened to distract me. This place was frozen somehow, stuck back in that 70s idealism that allowed for dreaming and romance and ignorance to the fact that we're all dying slow deaths as we breathe in the exhaust of our own industry.

Sliding my bottom along the wooden ledge, I found what I had come for. Iris' name screamed out at me from the wall. I could picture the shadow of her son, angry as he used a bolt to etch her into the church. I traced the letters with my fingers, shaking slightly with the cold and with the reality of what I was touching. Like reaching into a history book and feeling the texture of a soldiers uniform. I followed the path of the 'I' and leaned my forehead against the wall as if it could take the burden of my grief.

This is silly, I thought. *What am I doing?*

But I knew exactly what I was doing. I was tracing the truth of her. I was tracking her reality. I was discovering this miracle that came of my imagination and I was mourning the loss of the very thing I created.

I was weeping before I knew enough to stop. I

pressed myself against that wall and grieved into the wood, staining it with my tears.

She was gone. I had disappeared her. I pressed my palm hard against the carved imprint of her name as if I might press it onto my skin like a tattoo.

I want to take you with me everywhere.

Before I climbed down, I added my own name to the wall. Joseph and Grace had carved sins into the wood. They had made it their book of judgement. It was with anger and hurt that Joseph wrote his mother's name, accusatory in its rudimentary inscription—blaming Reverend Greene for her ultimate demise, though he had been the one who freed the nail that caused her death. Grace had carved the name of her high school boyfriend, Sherwin, the boy whose life was forever altered when Reverend Greene hit him with his car while rushing a fatally ill Iris to the hospital. I wasn't writing the Reverend's sins by putting my name beside Iris and Sherwin. I was writing my own, absolving Samuel Greene of any blame placed on him, taking it into myself, owning it, wrapping it up into who I was.

Because I am me.

But I am also Iris.

I am Samuel.

I am Joseph and Grace.

And everything is a circle.

chapter seven
black bird fly

"JUST YOU?" THE BIRD GIRL ASKED. SHE stood beside my table, coffee carafe in hand, a tiny stain on her white apron.

"Has the woman I was with yesterday stopped by?" I asked. A stupid question, but I couldn't help myself.

Bird raised an eyebrow and set the coffee pot down on the table. She lifted her arms to wind her hair into a quick bun, sticking it though with a yellow pencil. "Lady, you were here alone yesterday. You ordered that extra tea and no one drank it."

I fought a burning behind my eyes and blew out a loud puff of air, turning my head to stare out the window as I digested what I already knew. What I'd known with certainly since that moment she faded from my view. "I know," I whispered.

"You okay?" Bird asked.

Numbly, I shook my head.

She slid into the bench across from me and touched my hand with the tip of her finger. Her nails were painted black but her gesture was warm and I felt myself melting into a kindness I hadn't earned.

"Do you know anything of loss?" I asked, turning my wet gaze back to her face, her youth making me want to sob and order a milkshake at the same time.

The corner of her mouth turned up and I felt mesmerized by her beauty, the way it dressed her with a dark humility. She filled my empty cup from the carafe, slipped from the booth to grab another one off the counter, and then filled her own. We stared at each other through the steam. "I know many things about loss," she said. "Maybe I know all the things."

I added sugar and milk to my coffee while she sipped hers black. "But you're so young," I said.

"And you're so old?" The mirth in her voice invited me to match her smile with my own.

"Some days," I said.

"Me too."

"I'D LIKE TO WRITE YOUR STORY," I SAID, draining the last swallow of coffee.

"Why?"

I pulled the Moleskine from my bag, turning it open to the front page where I'd intended to write everything I learned from Iris. The blank paper stared back at me, mocking. *You've learned much and lost much and all of it is to be held close to your heart.* I flipped from the first page. I couldn't mar it. It would always belong to her.

A new page. A new story.

"No one would care," Bird said.

"You'd be surprised what people care about."

"You like to write tragedy?"

"Shakespeare grew famous on tragedies."

She laughed.

"You know of loss." I said. "But do you also know of redemption?"

She leaned back in her seat, pulled the pencil from her hair and dragged my notebook across the table. *Black Bird* she wrote across the top of the page. And below that: *No Hope.*

"You don't mean that," I said.

She laughed and added two more letters.

"*Know hope,*" I read. "That's beautiful."

"Not beautiful," she said. "But it's a reason to keep living, even in all the loss."

"Do you believe in heaven?" I asked.

She shrugged. "Flowers have a soul in every leaf."

"What do you mean?"

"God is a dandelion. I watched him die."

"Why are you telling me this?"

"Because it doesn't matter, does it? You're not really here. You're out there. Somewhere. You've never been here. This isn't your world, though in a sense, you are its god."

"Why are you able to accept that?"

"Because you let me." She reached across the table and grabbed my mug, picking it up with her own and taking it behind the counter. "It will be dark," she called back to me.

"What will?"

"My story."

"I know."

"But you like that, don't you?"

"Part of me does."

"Why?"

"Because we're all broken in little ways."

"Yes. Or big ways." She untied her apron and used the little sink beside the coffee machine to dampen the cloth. She scrubbed it where the stain had been.

"What do you mean?"

"Just wait until you meet my mother." She

paused, glancing across the café to the booth that housed the same big man that had sat there the last time. Her eyelids fluttered and she took a deep breath before returning her gaze to me. "And my father," she added. She hung her apron up on a hook beside the swinging door to the kitchen. "I'm outta here, Likely," she called to the other waitress across the room."

"Yep—see you!"

"Bye, Raven," she called to the big man and his apple crisp.

His shoulders straightened and a sad little smile turned up the corner of his tired face. "Bye bye, Birdie." He balanced a two dollar coin on his thumb nail. "Don't forget your tip. Likely didn't earn nothing from me."

"Hey!" Likely retorted from behind the counter.

"Nobody's filled this coffee cup tonight but Bird."

"Yeah okay."

He flicked his thumb against his forefinger, sending the coin flying.

Bird snatched it out of the air. "Thanks, Mr. Wolfe."

She stopped by me one last time, resting her fingertips against the edge of my table. "Want to hear something really sad?"

I reached out and grasped her fingers, winding

my own around them like I was sewing stitches to mend something torn.

Her eyes were soft and she let me hold her hand as she slid in beside me. "I asked a Walmart cashier to be my mother."

The hurt she piled on that confession pushed a puff of air from my throat.

"She was just so kind to me. And pretty. And I thought she was made of the stuff that would make a good mother. So I asked her. But then she looked at me with this tragic smile and I felt so stupid."

"Everyone deserves a kind mother."

"When a baby bird falls from the nest, nine times out of ten, they'll die."

"But you didn't die. You're not going to."

"Everyone dies. It's living that's the real test." She let go of my hand and stood. "I have to go." She pressed a finger onto my open notebook and the words she'd written. "Don't forget," she said. "It's up to you."

She stood and turned to slip her arm into the sleeve of her coat. Overhead light caught her shoulder, shining through the thin fabric of her white blouse, showing the shadow of her bra... and something else... a tattoo? She saw me staring and grabbed at her shoulder, twisting her head to peer back over it so she might see what I was looking at.

"Ah," she said. "You might as well know. You'll find out anyway." She undid the top few buttons on her shirt and pulled it down from the back to bare her shoulder. The font was pretty, curving across her shoulder, following the shape of her body. *'Sin of the Father'*.

"What does it mean?" I asked, my mind flashing to the memory of Iris and her carved thigh.

She smiled sadly and I glanced across the restaurant to see the big man... Raven?... Mr. Wolfe?... looking back at us with wet eyes. "You'll see," she said quietly, pulling her shirt back up to cover her shoulder before doing up the buttons and pulling on her coat.

I watched her leave, feeling a shift in the air and in myself. I traced her lettering in my notebook and knew her story would be the next one I told; that I couldn't rest until I'd done it; that on some level it mattered in a way that would shift my universe.

I placed my pen beneath her words and I began to write.

chapter eight
strong shoes

THERE CAME THE BRUSH OF SOMETHING soft over my face. Like cotton. Or feathers. A breath? I stirred beneath the quilt my grandmother made me, coming to full consciousness before I even thought to question the presence of my grandmother's quilt in a motel room. My heart pulsed in my chest—a rude, unnatural rush that felt like a rip tide, like I might stop breathing, like I might drown at any moment. I scrambled back against the headboard and closed my eyes, willing myself to settle.

I was in my bed. *My* bed. In my home.

I was a long way from Fallmoore.

Iris?

There was still a hint of her scent on the air. A flutter of something white across the wall at the end of my bed.

I didn't remember returning home.

I slid back down, pulling the quilt over my head.

So that's it. A dream.

I shut my eyes and tried to catch up with her, watching the hem of her skirt drift around a corner, always just beyond my reach, a shadow without a shadow.

Nothing lasts. Even great love.

I remembered my notebook. I peeked out from under the blanket and saw it laying on my side table. I reached over, fingers shaking, and let it fall open.

The pages were empty. I flipped through, feeling a great sense of loss.

No!

But then, on the second page. Four words stared back at me.

Black Bird
kNow Hope

It was not my handwriting.

I sat up and whipped back the quilt, swinging my legs over the edge of the bed as I traced the letters. I felt their legacy and impossibility beneath my fingertips.

My eyes fell on my shoes sitting in the corner. They were covered in dust. One had a few little evergreen needles clinging to it by a single drop of tree sap.

And there beside them sat a pair of sandals that weren't my own. Clean but worn, like they'd walked miles to find me.

Iris?

I looked back at those words in my notebook. *Black Bird.*

I knew what I needed to do.

AUTHOR'S NOTE

This novella is what happens when an author is so in love with a character that they struggle to let go. I am thankful to Iris for indulging me in this cathartic journey, and I am grateful for anyone that came along for the ride. It's fascinating and morbidly beautiful that an invention of my own design can dig itself so deeply beneath my skin.

I need to thank every reader who allowed themselves to be caught up in the world of *The Church in the Wildwood*, who reached out and asked for more, who encouraged me to chase after the story, and ultimately allowed me to unlock an entire series I'm itching to share.

Thank you to the dedicated beta-readers who helped me bring this little indulgence to its ultimate potential: William F. Aicher, Heidi Eastman, Lisa Gilbert, Pamela Hopwood, Debbie Kaster, Patricia Manale, Luke McLaughlin, Michelle McLaughlin, and Geraldine Mac Donald.

Thank you, as always, to my Writer's Jam girls for being an endless source of encouragement; to my children for forgiving our less-than-perfect home; and to my husband, Scott, for crying at the *Wildwood* book launch.

SOUNDTRACK

Catch the emotions of this little story by listening through The Ghost of Iris Carver Soundtrack, curated by the author.

1. **Spaceman** *by Francois Klark*
2. **Talking to Ghosts** *by Bittersweet Machines*
3. **I Still Haven't Found What I'm Looking For** *by U2*
4. **This Town** *by Niall Horan*
5. **Oh God Come Back** *by Bass Lions*
6. **You Carry Me** *by Ash & Bloom*
7. **Weighty Ghost** *by Wintersleep*
8. **Leave A Mark** *by Hydrogen Sea*
9. **Call It Dreaming** *by Iron & Wine*
10. **Treaty** *by Leonard Cohen*
11. **A Case of You** *by Joni Mitchell*
12. **All of Me** *by John Legend*

Also by Alanna Rusnak

When We Were Young (2013)

Eve Undone (2016)

Kissing Johnny (2016)

The Church in the Wildwood (2017)

Just Words Volume 1 (contributing author) (2017)

and coming soon

Black Bird
(continue for a sneak preview)

FROM THE AUTHOR OF THE CHURCH IN THE WILDWOOD
black bird
the Fallmoore Chronicles
same town | different heartbreak
all Bird wants is
a chance to fly away
ALANNA RUSNAK

chapter
one

MOTHER WAS ALWAYS NICEST AFTER SHE'D taken her medicine. As the plunger sank, her eyes would soften and she would nearly love me for a moment as she brushed my hair idly, her broken fingernails catching in its gold, whispering beneath her breath about how Joni Mitchell was the only person who would ever truly understand her.

It bruised her arm: there where she stuck herself with happily-ever-after; there where a silver line pushed into the midnight blue beneath skin so white and pale it seemed to glow like a ghost with its own preternatural light.

I knew the truth of it. I knew her lies. I knew her brokenness. I knew that she was like a mirror smashed by an angry fist and no matter how long I tried and how careful I was and how perfectly I fit those pieces back together, the reflection would always be distorted and cracked—a weak remembrance of the beauty she was long before my own beginnings.

I would never be enough.

REVEREND SAUL'S OLD CHICKEN SHED spilled a mournful shadow across the lawn he cut with a reel mower and a straw Panama. We were sleeping there two weeks before he even realized and invited us to stay with him in the little white-sided parsonage.

My mother had laughed at him. "Get a grip, old man," she had said. "I'm not nobody's maid."

He hadn't even winced. Just brought out a little oil heater that ticked through the night, an old brown microwave, and a little white humming fridge that somehow always had milk.

WE WERE LYING ON OUR BACKS, THE GRASS tickling out necks with ripe sweet fingers that dared us to hope. Mother was stretching up, up, up, weaving her hands through air that smelled like summer, as if she could capture the scent and seal it into herself, as if that would make her matter.

I was tracing my finger along the bows of the wind, following the lazy maze of clouds, their lines and curves, their tones of forever. "What colour is God?" I asked, my voice blending with the rustle of leaves and the whisper of barley in the field beyond the yard.

She turned to me slowly, gazing out through the wasted window that had closed over her eyes, the ones that seemed thick and wet and reflected me back doubly big and shining. "God's not no colour," she said. "He's just bright and violent like those clouds. He ain't nothing..." and she squeezed a fist and held it where it blocked a cloud shaped like a seal. "...Nothing to not be worth what it takes to save a girl from a monster..."

My back started to hurt—an ache that became a slow burn, melding through my heart and down into my belly, just like every other time she started talking about my daddy.

I rolled over onto my stomach, burrowing my chin into my folded arms, thinking hard about the sun on the back of my sweater and how its fingered rays were slowly kneading away the perpetual pain of my father.

"I just thought he had to be a colour, is all," I

said.

"You need that, Bird? You need him to have a colour?"

And I really thought I did because I was smothering in the black and white of my world and if God was as grey as I was we might as well turn it in and tip the oil furnace over while we slept.

"Fine." She released the fist that had tried to curb all that bright violence, sent it out into chaos with a sigh, and felled that hand like a tree onto sod, rending from its seeding a dollop of sunshine and dropping it before my nose. "Here," she said. "Here's God." She stood, cut grass clinging to her grey joggers. "Flowers have a soul in every leaf!" Her voice was sharp and mocking as she brushed the cuttings from her leg. She weaved back to the shed to nap upon the Walmart air mattress that took up more than half the cement floor. The door slammed shut and another strip of paint flaked off and fell to the rotting step.

I stared down at the dandelion, at its chubby face, at its tones of sunshine, at its woven grace and tender lines and I knew the truth of it the moment I breathed in that yellow breath of summer. "Hello, God," I whispered.

THE CHICKEN SHED WAS SMALL, SET UPON

the parsonage lawn like someone forgot it there—like it had been tossed off the train that once ran beside Highway 11 from Harridan Point every Tuesday and Thursday.

Cedar shingles clung like barnacles to the shed facade, resting one upon the other like sad fall leaves, the dull colour of an angry hurricane. A low eave hung over the door, its peeling paint as red as a barn, the roof protected in grey metal sheeting that caught the sun and kept us warm inside.

This was no home sweet home. It was nothing but a ceiling and a secret, wrapped up tight and bitter in the parish of Eastern Bodensee at the north end of Fallmoore, a nowhere town with secrets of its own—too many to ever concern itself with mine.

I lived in the back corner, where the wall faced the barley field and its early morning tractor rumbles. Mother strung a wire and hung a tarp she stole from the neighbours woodpile to separate us so she didn't always have to look at my face.

Too often my familiar features reminded her that she hated herself.

I had two blankets, two pillows, and one grimy window barred with chicken wire. My wall was floor to ceiling nesting boxes. I spent a whole week hiding behind the tarp, cleaning them of mouldy straw and dusty droppings that turned to ash when I tried to wipe them away.

One box held my jeans, one my shirts, one my socks and underwear.

The others stood empty.

A testament to my life.

They were where I stored my dreams of something better.

I TIPTOED PAST MOTHER TO GET TO MY private corner. Her mouth hung open and a small puddle discoloured the pillow by her face. Her finger twitched. When she sleeps, she is soft. Sometimes I wished she would sleep forever.

I had a tin can rescued from Saul's recycling and filled with icy water from the garden hose. I set the can in the nesting box nearest the window and settled God inside. He flopped against the edge and I worried he might hurt himself against the raw cut tin but he seemed okay. Even seemed to turn his head a little so he could soak more sun through the dirty glass.

"You'll be safe here," I promised, and he nodded a little with the wind from my breath.

"I think she's broken," I whispered.

He nodded his head.

"I think, someday, every piece will have fallen away and there will be nothing left except her paintings on my wings... She says I'm a *fairigon*, you know. That's part fairy and part dragon. She says I am of evil but I think maybe she is... She thinks she's an angel but Peri really means 'a fallen angel'... there's no heaven in her heart, only sadness... I think maybe I'm the oldest fifteen year old in the whole world..."

One tiny shock of yellow fell from his face like a sunshine tear. It drifted like a feather and I traced its path with a wish for freedom from this stale living. It settled against the worn wood, a tattoo of promise.

I took it from its resting place and I ate it.

ABOUT THE AUTHOR

Alanna Rusnak lives on a small patch of untameable land in mid-western Ontario with her three children, husband, and an over-weight cat. Fuelled by copious amounts of caffeine and chocolate, she writes fiction and creative non-fiction from within her tiny study, fantasizing about meeting her characters.

Facebook *facebook.com/alannarusnakauthor*
Goodreads *goodreads.com/alannarusnak*
Instagram *@alannarusnak*
Twitter *@alannarusnak*

Subscribe for updates at **alannarusnak.com** for news of upcoming releases, press events, and the status of various projects.

If you've enjoyed this, or other books by Alanna, please consider leaving a review anywhere her books are sold or promoted (Amazon, Goodreads, Barnes & Noble, Chapters Indigo, etc.)